P9-BZI-594

If I Didn't Have You

To Sol—I wouldn't be me if I didn't have you
—*A. K.*

To all the lovely agents at the Bright Group,
but especially to my agent, Alli (Gator) Brydon
—*C. R.*

SIMON & SCHUSTER BOOKS FOR YOUNG READERS
An imprint of Simon & Schuster Children's Publishing Division
1230 Avenue of the Americas, New York, New York 10020

For information about special discounts for bulk purchases, please contact Simon & Schuster Special Sales
at 1-866-506-1949 or business@simonandschuster.com.
The Simon & Schuster Speakers Bureau can bring authors to your live event.
For more information or to book an event, contact the Simon & Schuster Speakers Bureau
at 1-866-248-3049 or visit our website at www.simonspeakers.com.
Book design by Laurent Linn
The text for this book was set in Yourz Truly.
The illustrations for this book were rendered digitally.
Manufactured in China
0118 SCP
First Edition
10 9 8 7 6 5 4 3 2 1
Library of Congress Cataloging-in-Publication Data
Names: Katz, Alan, author. | Robertson, Chris, 1958– illustrator.
Title: If I didn't have you / Alan Katz ; illustrated by Chris Robertson.
Other titles: If I did not have you
Description: First edition. | New York : Simon & Schuster Books for Young Readers, [2018] | Summary: "A father and son spend the day together detailing all of the things they could have...if they didn't have each other. In the end, they both decide that candy for dinner every night or a personal butler is no substitute for a father or a son"— Provided by publisher.
Identifiers: LCCN 2015026686 | ISBN 9781416978794 (hardcover) | ISBN 9781481476409 (ebook)
Subjects: | CYAC: Father and child—Fiction.
Classification: LCC PZ7.K15669 If 2018 | DDC [E]—dc23 LC record available at http://lccn.loc.gov/2015026686

If I Didn't Have You

Alan Katz

ILLUSTRATED BY Chris Robertson

SIMON & SCHUSTER BOOKS FOR YOUNG READERS

NEW YORK LONDON TORONTO SYDNEY NEW DELHI

"How come you don't have a car like *that*, Dad?" Mike asked as a sleek Speedster roared down their street.

"Well, there are three people in this family, and that car only seats two," his dad replied.

"So you could have a custom-built sports car with racing stripes . . . if you didn't have me?" asked Mike.

"I wouldn't trade you for anything, son," Dad answered.

"And I suppose I *could* drive that car . . . if I didn't have you. But I'd rather have you."

"Well, *I* could stay up until midnight every night," said Mike, "if I didn't have you."

"I imagine you could," his dad replied. "Yes, you probably could."

"And I would never have to clean
my room . . . if I didn't have you."

"Know what else?" Mike said.
"I could eat candy for every meal . . .
if I didn't have you!"

"If you did that, you wouldn't have to brush your teeth, either—because you wouldn't *have* any teeth!" Mike's dad said.

Mike couldn't decide if that would be a good thing or not.

"Hey, Dad, what could you do if you didn't have me?" Mike asked.

"I suppose I could take sky-diving
lessons . . . if I didn't have you.
But I'd rather have you."

"Well, Dad, I could stay home from school and play video games all day . . . if I didn't have you."

"I could use your room to house my personal butler . . . if I didn't have you," Dad said.

"I could adopt as many pets as
I want . . . if I didn't have you."

"Well, I could take a year-long journey around the globe in a hot air balloon . . . if I didn't have you," Dad offered.

"But you'd rather have me?" Mike asked.

"Absolutely," Dad said.

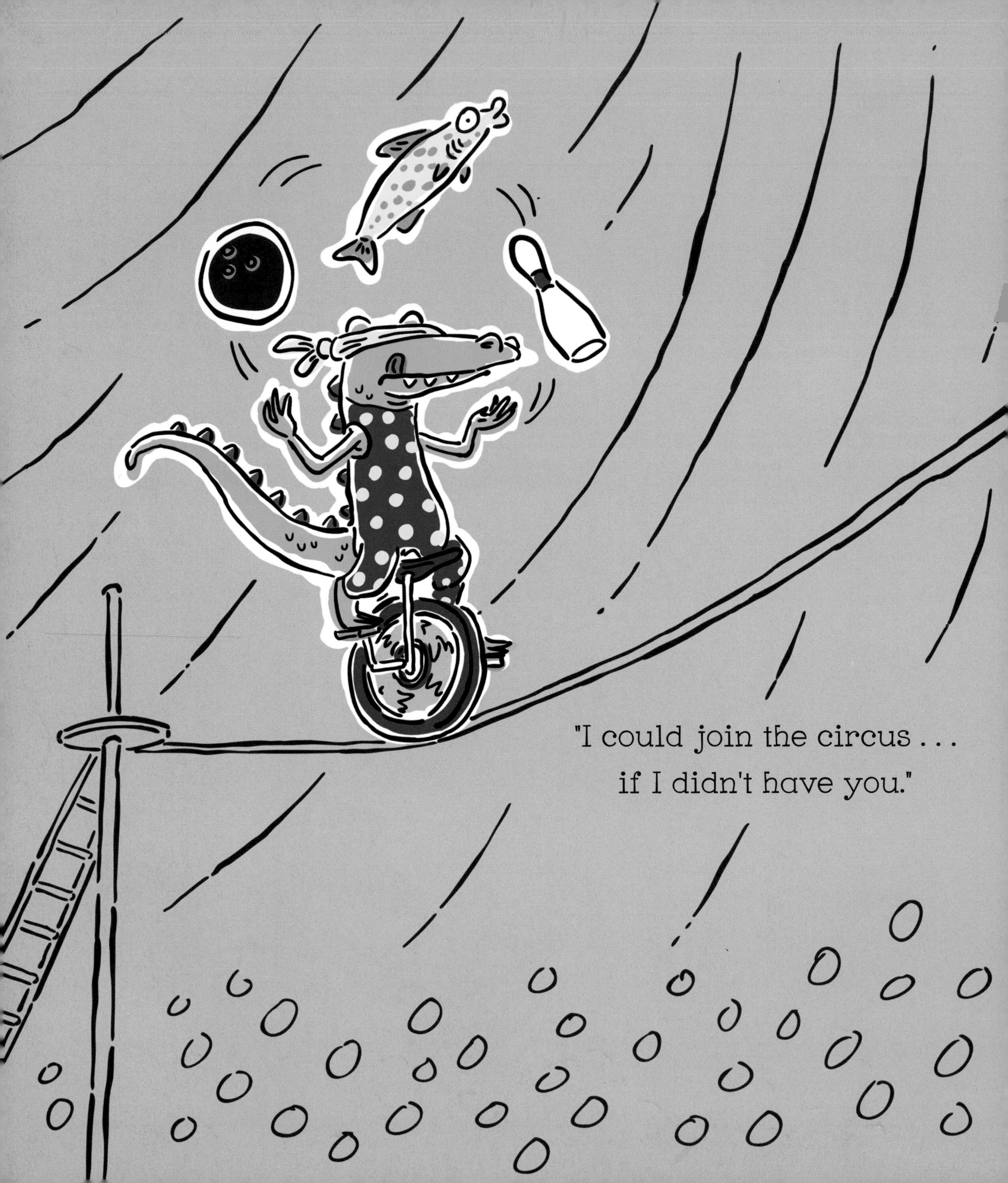
"I could join the circus . . .
if I didn't have you."

"I could pursue my dream
of becoming a rock star . . .
if I didn't have you."

"I could put my bare, stinky feet on the dining room table during dinner . . . if I didn't have you."

"Why would you want to do that?"
Dad asked.

"Oh yeah, never mind,"
Mike said.

"But . . . I could play really
loud music and dance like
crazy whenever I felt like it . . .
if I didn't have you."

"You can dance like crazy
with me," Dad said.

"Really?" Mike asked.

"Of course!"

So Mike put on his favorite song as loud as the stereo would play it, and he and Dad danced and danced and danced and danced throughout the house.

When the song
was over, they
played it again.
And again.
And again.

"Dad," Mike said as he huffed and puffed when the dancing stopped.

"I didn't really mean I'd rather stay up all night and watch TV all the time and have nonstop candy and join the circus and everything."

"I know," said Dad. "And, Mike, I didn't really mean I'd prefer the butler and the hot air balloon trip and all the other stuff."

Mike smiled. "I'd rather have you, Dad."

"I'd rather have you, Mike."

Then Mom walked in. She saw the couch where the chair used to be, and the cushions on the kitchen counter, and the lamp lying on the floor.

She slapped her cheeks in surprise and said,
"I'd have a neat, calm, peaceful home . . .
if I didn't have you!"

"But you'd rather have us, right, dear?" Dad said.

"Yeah, Mom, you'd rather have us, right?" Mike echoed. "Right?"

Finally Mom said,
"Yes, I'd rather
have you."

"Of course, what I'd *really* like is . . .
a custom-built sports car with racing stripes!"